THE ALL NEW!

BATMAN

THE BRAVE AND THE BOLD

STONE ARCH BOOKS
a capstone imprint

STONE ARCH BOOKS™

Published in 2015 by Stone Arch Books
A Capstone Imprint
1710 Roe Crest Drive
North Mankato, MN 56003
www.capstonepub.com

Originally published by DC Comics in the U.S. in single magazine form as The All-New Batman: The Brave and the Bold #2
Original U.S. Editor: Scott Peterson

DC Comics
1700 Broadway, New York, NY 10019
A Warner Bros. Entertainment Company

Library of Congress Cataloging-in-Publication Data
Fisch, Sholly, author.
That holiday feeling / Sholly Fisch, writer ; Rick Burchett, penciler ; Dan Davis, inker ; Heroic Age, colorist.
pages cm. -- [The all-new Batman: the brave and the bold ; 2]
"Originally published by DC Comics in the U.S. in single magazine form as The All-New Batman: The Brave and the Bold #2."
"Batman created by Bob Kane."
Summary: When the Psycho-Pirate hurls Gotham into an abyss of its darkest emotions, even Batman is trapped in deepest despair and only Captain Marvel can help the Dark Knight save the city.
ISBN 978-1-4342-9659-7 [library binding]
1. Batman [Fictitious character]--Comic books, strips, etc. 2. Batman [Fictitious character]--Juvenile fiction. 3. Superheroes--Comic books, strips, etc. 4. Superheroes--Juvenile fiction. 5. Supervillains--Comic books, strips, etc. 6. Supervillains--Juvenile fiction. 7. Graphic novels. [1. Graphic novels. 2. Superheroes--Fiction. 3. Supervillains--Fiction.] I. Burchett, Rick, illustrator. II. Kane, Bob, creator. III. Title.

PZ7.7.F57Ho 2015
741.5'973--dc23

2014028251

STONE ARCH BOOKS
Ashley C. Andersen Zantop Publisher
Michael Dahl Editorial Director
Eliza Leahy Editor
Heather Kindseth Creative Director
Bob Lentz Art Director
Peggie Carley Designer
Katy LaVigne Production Specialist

Printed in China by Nordica.
0914/CA21401510
092014 008470NORDS15

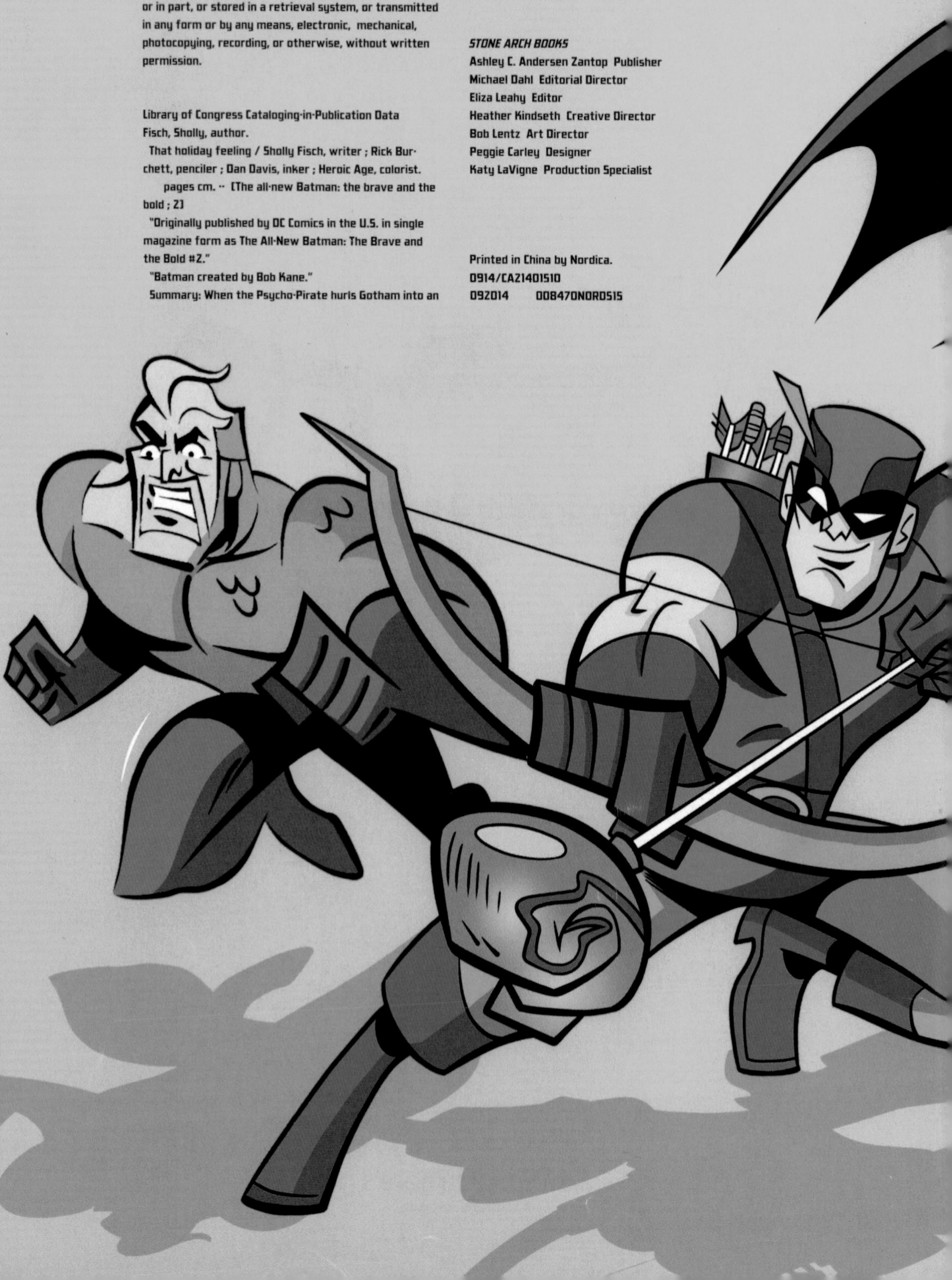

THE ALL NEW!

BATMAN
THE BRAVE AND THE BOLD

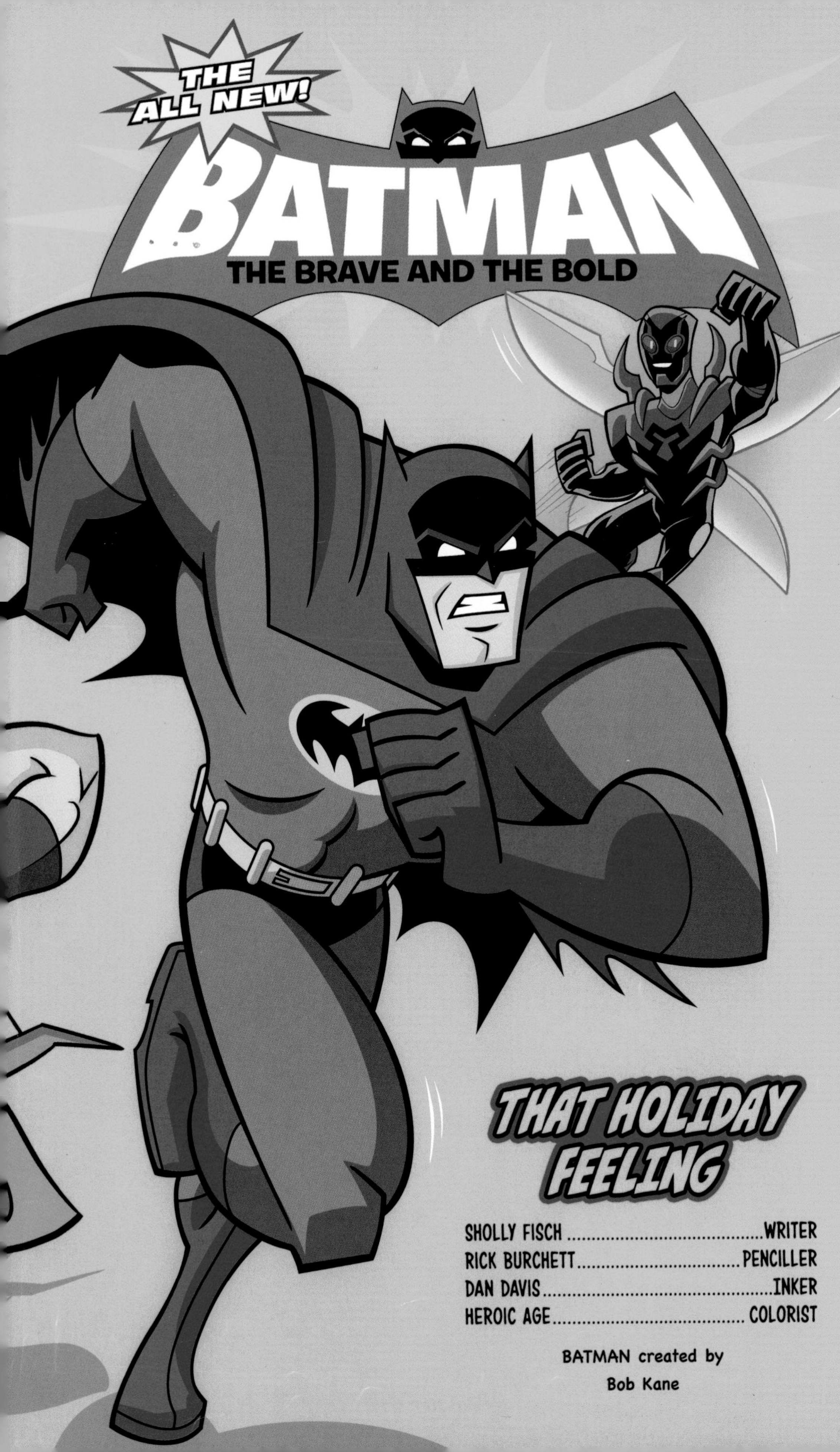

THAT HOLIDAY FEELING

SHOLLY FISCH ....WRITER
RICK BURCHETT..................................PENCILLER
DAN DAVIS..INKER
HEROIC AGE.. COLORIST

BATMAN created by
Bob Kane

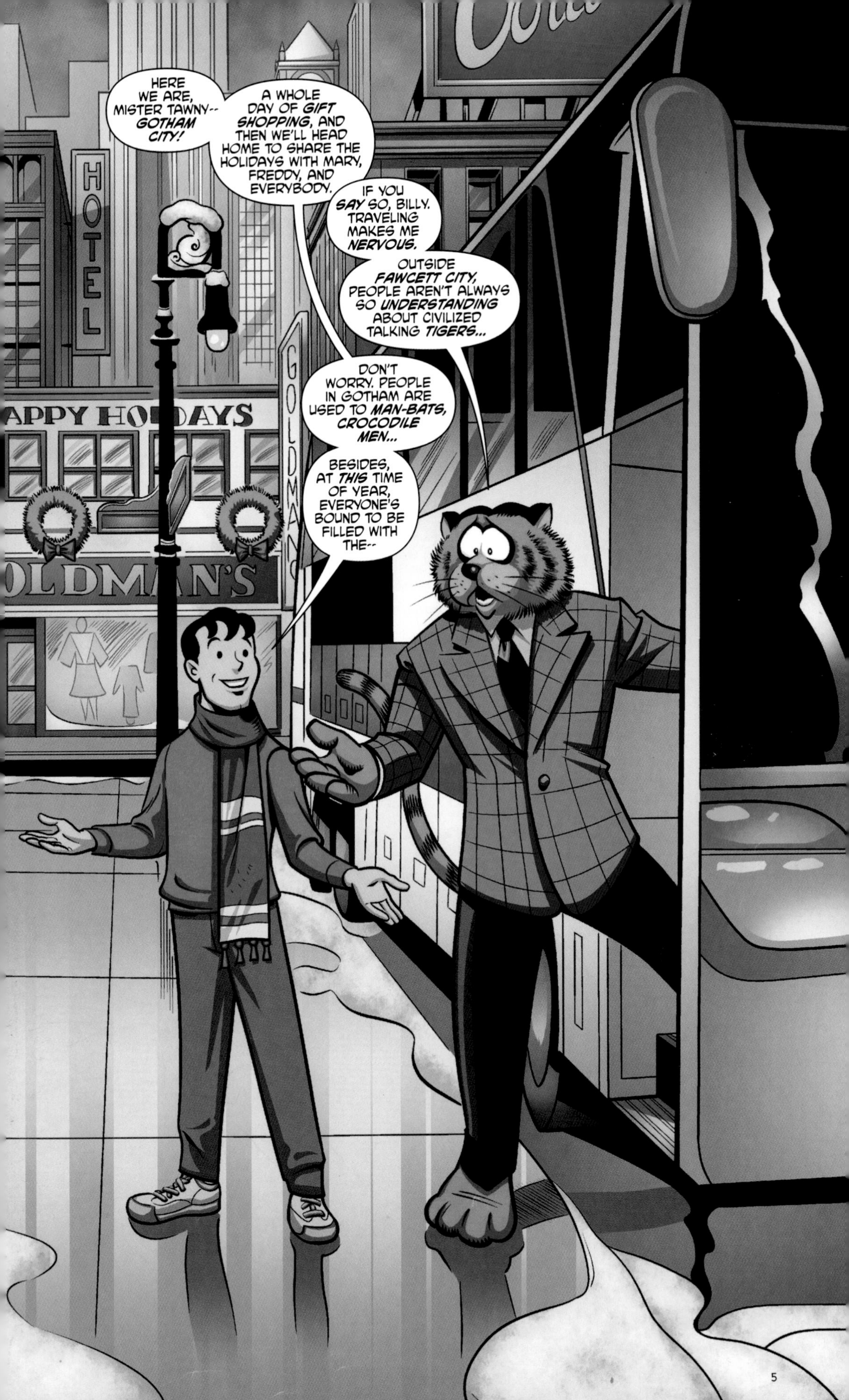
HERE WE ARE, MISTER TAWNY-- GOTHAM CITY!
A WHOLE DAY OF GIFT SHOPPING, AND THEN WE'LL HEAD HOME TO SHARE THE HOLIDAYS WITH MARY, FREDDY, AND EVERYBODY.
IF YOU SAY SO, BILLY. TRAVELING MAKES ME NERVOUS.
OUTSIDE FAWCETT CITY, PEOPLE AREN'T ALWAYS SO UNDERSTANDING ABOUT CIVILIZED TALKING TIGERS...
DON'T WORRY. PEOPLE IN GOTHAM ARE USED TO MAN-BATS, CROCODILE MEN...
BESIDES, AT THIS TIME OF YEAR, EVERYONE'S BOUND TO BE FILLED WITH THE--
HOTEL
APPY HO DAYS
GOLDMAN'S
OLDMAN'S

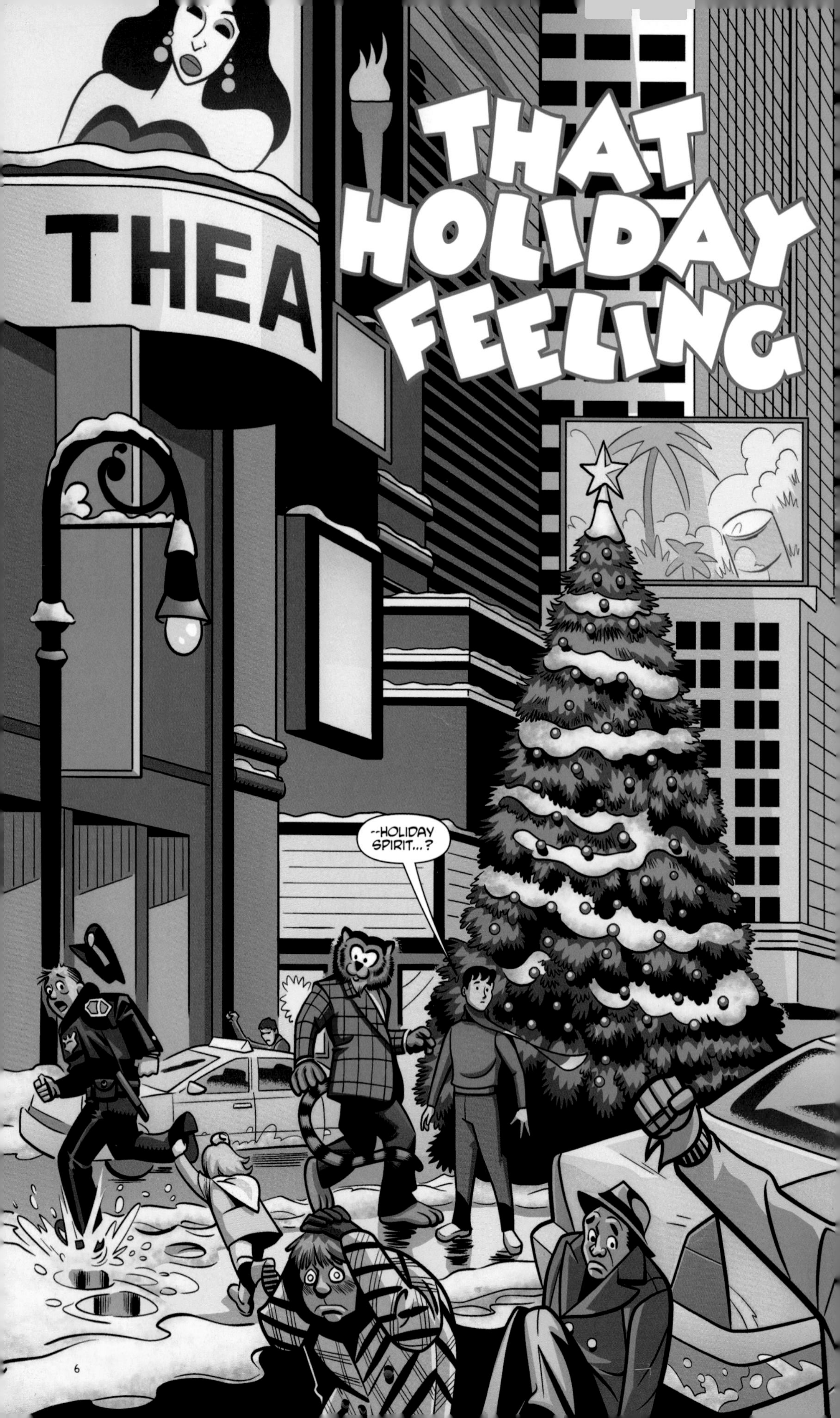
THEA
THAT HOLIDAY FEELING
--HOLIDAY SPIRIT...?

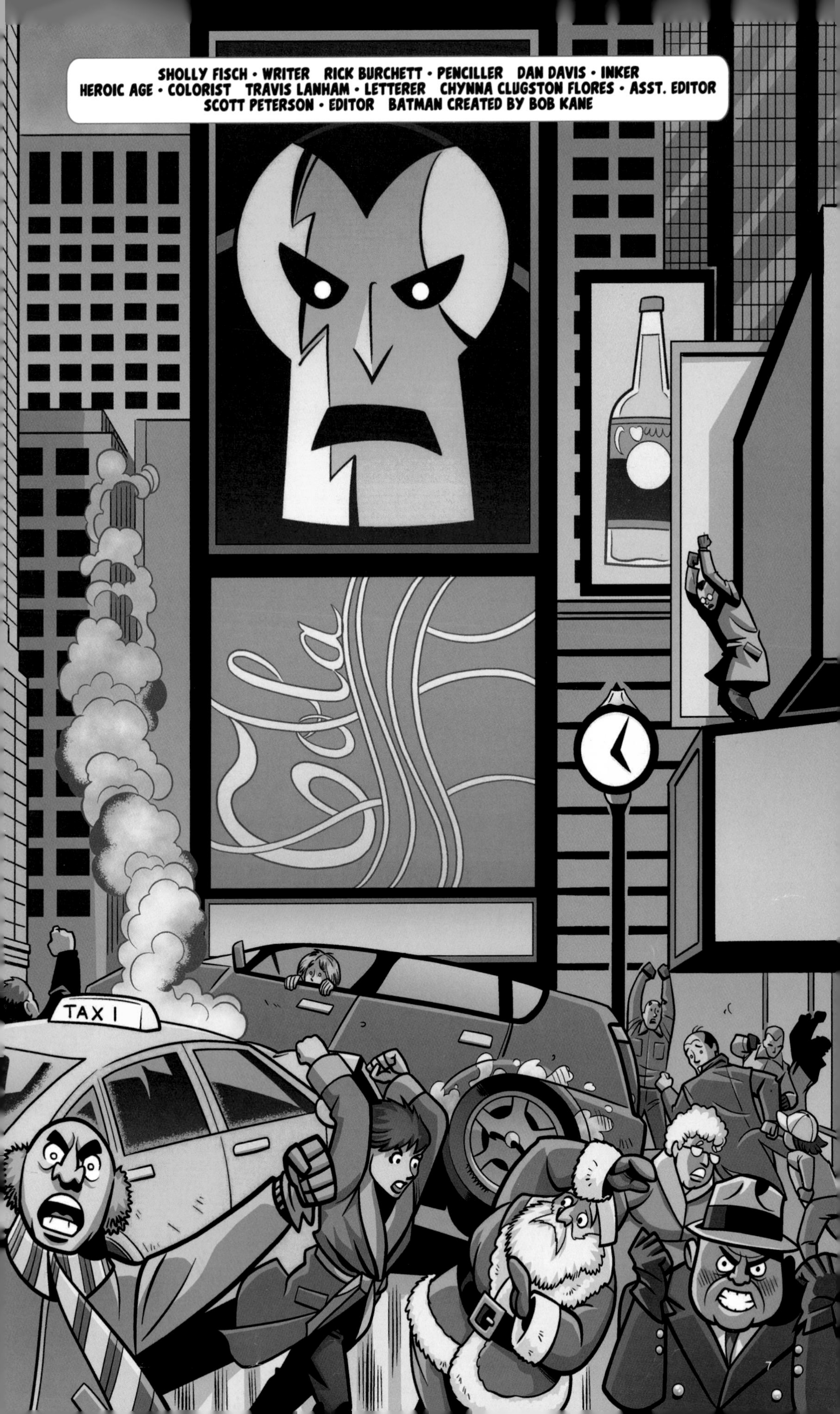
SHOLLY FISCH • WRITER RICK BURCHETT • PENCILLER DAN DAVIS • INKER
HEROIC AGE • COLORIST TRAVIS LANHAM • LETTERER CHYNNA CLUGSTON FLORES • ASST. EDITOR
SCOTT PETERSON • EDITOR BATMAN CREATED BY BOB KANE
TAXI

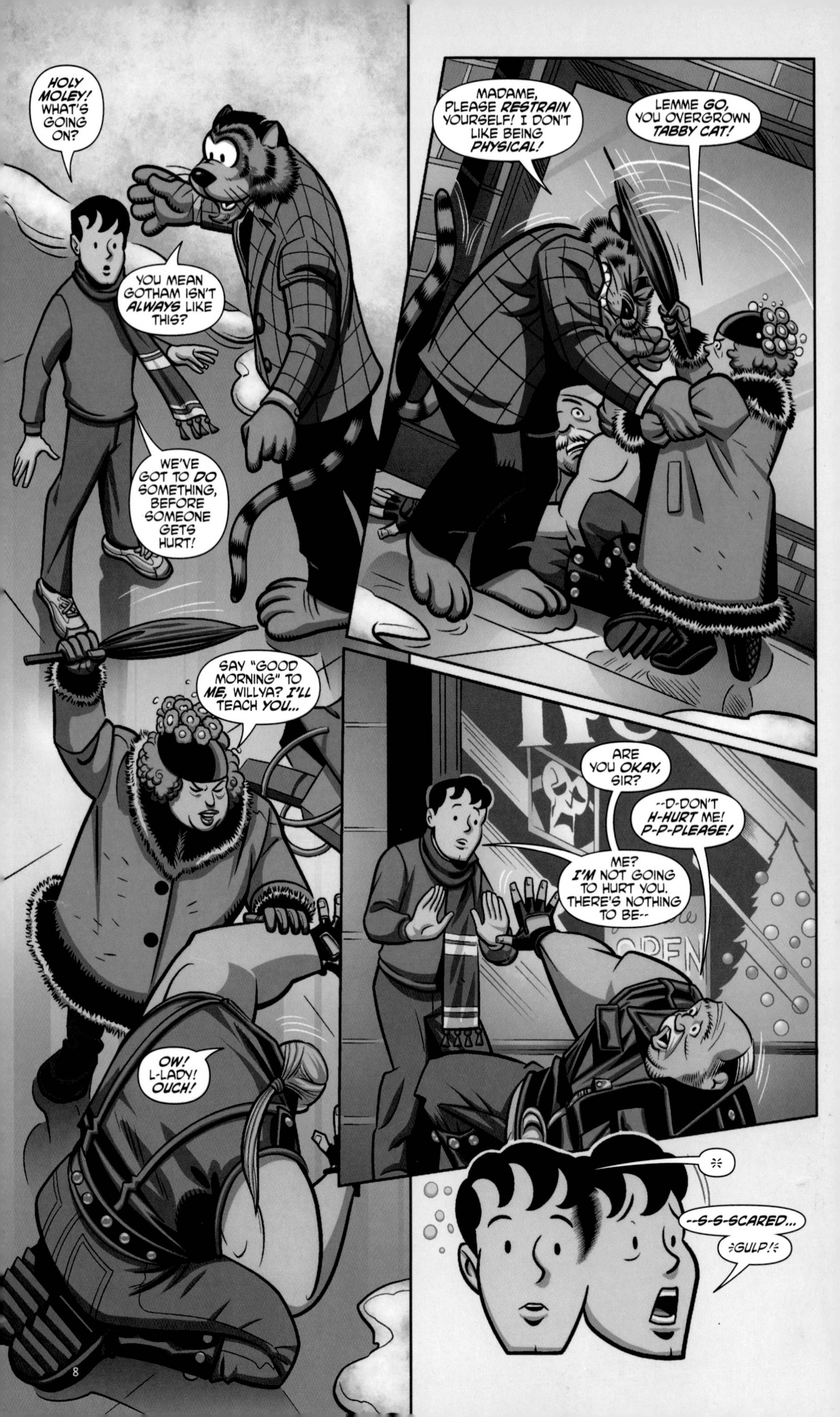
HOLY MOLEY! WHAT'S GOING ON?
YOU MEAN GOTHAM ISN'T ALWAYS LIKE THIS?
WE'VE GOT TO DO SOMETHING, BEFORE SOMEONE GETS HURT!
MADAME, PLEASE RESTRAIN YOURSELF! I DON'T LIKE BEING PHYSICAL!
LEMME GO, YOU OVERGROWN TABBY CAT!
SAY "GOOD MORNING" TO ME, WILLYA? I'LL TEACH YOU...
OW! L-LADY! OUCH!
ARE YOU OKAY, SIR?
--D-DON'T H-HURT ME! P-P-PLEASE!
ME? I'M NOT GOING TO HURT YOU. THERE'S NOTHING TO BE--
OPEN
--S-S-SCARED...
GULP!

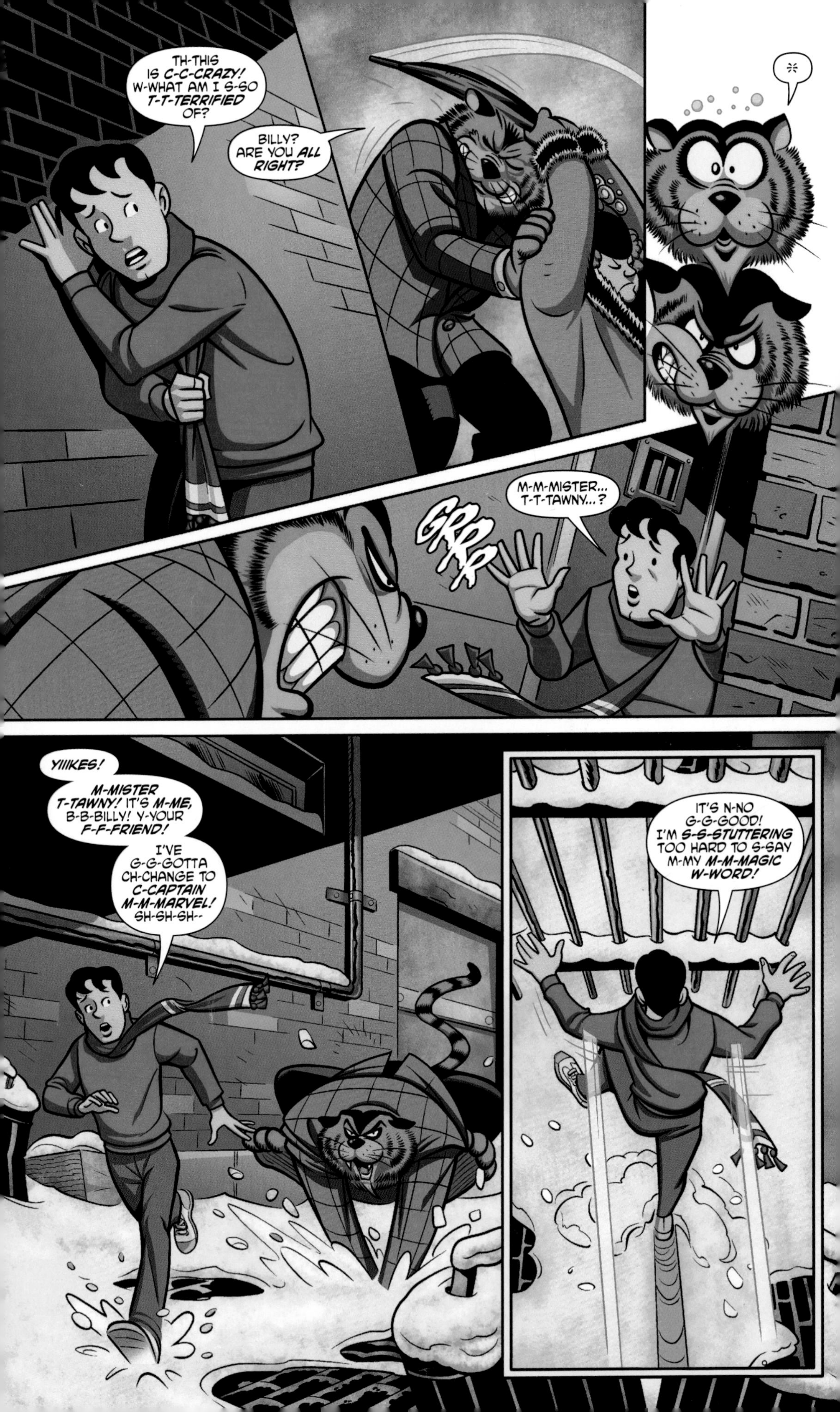

TH-THIS IS C-C-CRAZY! W-WHAT AM I S-SO T-T-TERRIFIED OF?
BILLY? ARE YOU ALL RIGHT?
*
M-M-MISTER... T-T-TAWNY...?
GRRR
YIIIKES!
M-MISTER T-TAWNY! IT'S M-ME, B-B-BILLY! Y-YOUR F-F-FRIEND!
I'VE G-G-GOTTA CH-CHANGE TO C-CAPTAIN M-M-MARVEL! SH-SH-SH--
IT'S N-NO G-G-GOOD! I'M S-S-STUTTERING TOO HARD TO S-SAY M-MY M-M-MAGIC W-WORD!

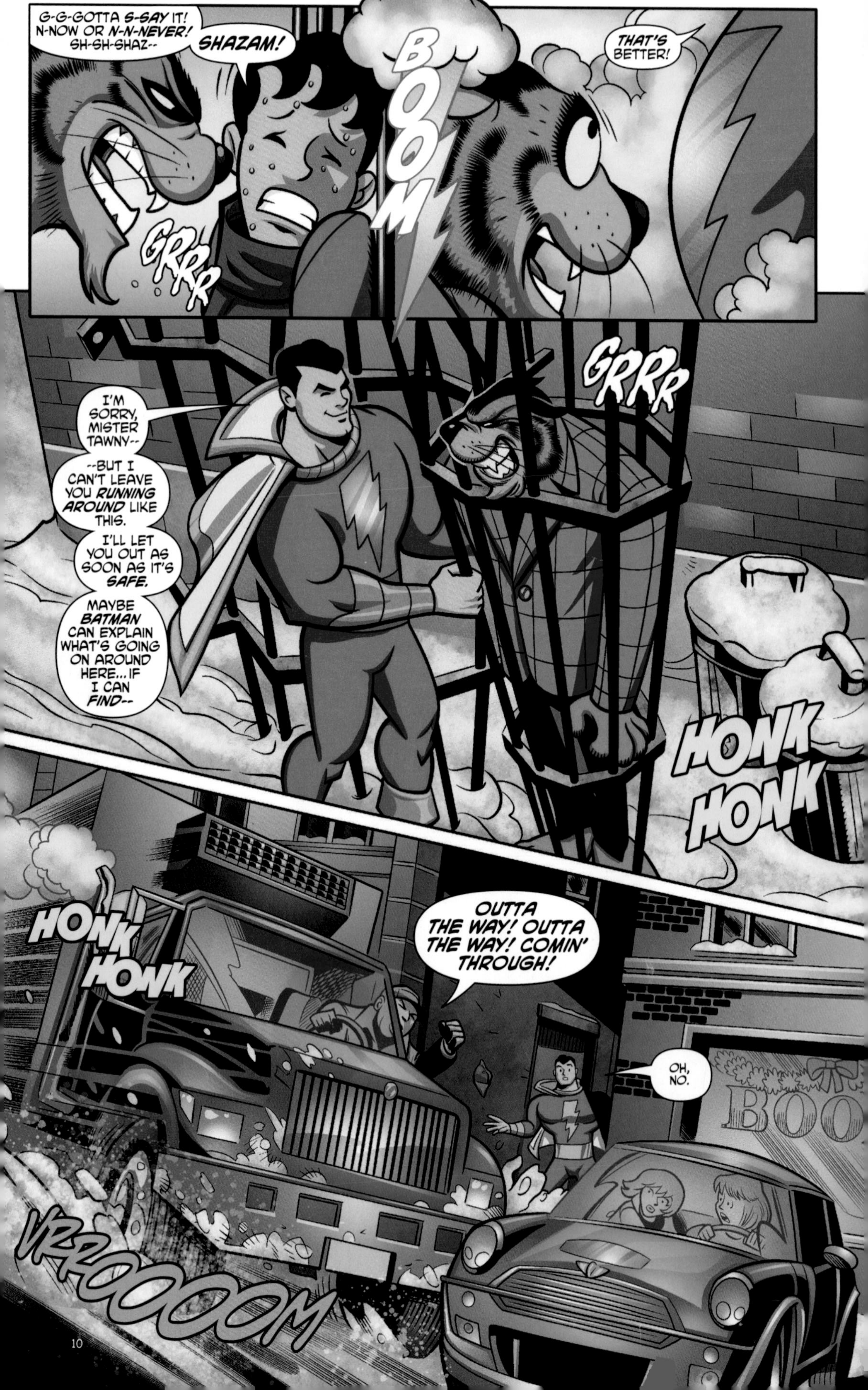
G-G-GOTTA S-SAY IT! N-NOW OR N-N-NEVER! SH-SH-SHAZ--
SHAZAM!
BOOOM
GRRR
THAT'S BETTER!
GRRR
I'M SORRY, MISTER TAWNY--
--BUT I CAN'T LEAVE YOU RUNNING AROUND LIKE THIS.
I'LL LET YOU OUT AS SOON AS IT'S SAFE.
MAYBE BATMAN CAN EXPLAIN WHAT'S GOING ON AROUND HERE...IF I CAN FIND--
HONK HONK
HONK HONK
OUTTA THE WAY! OUTTA THE WAY! COMIN' THROUGH!
OH, NO.
BOO
VRROOOOM

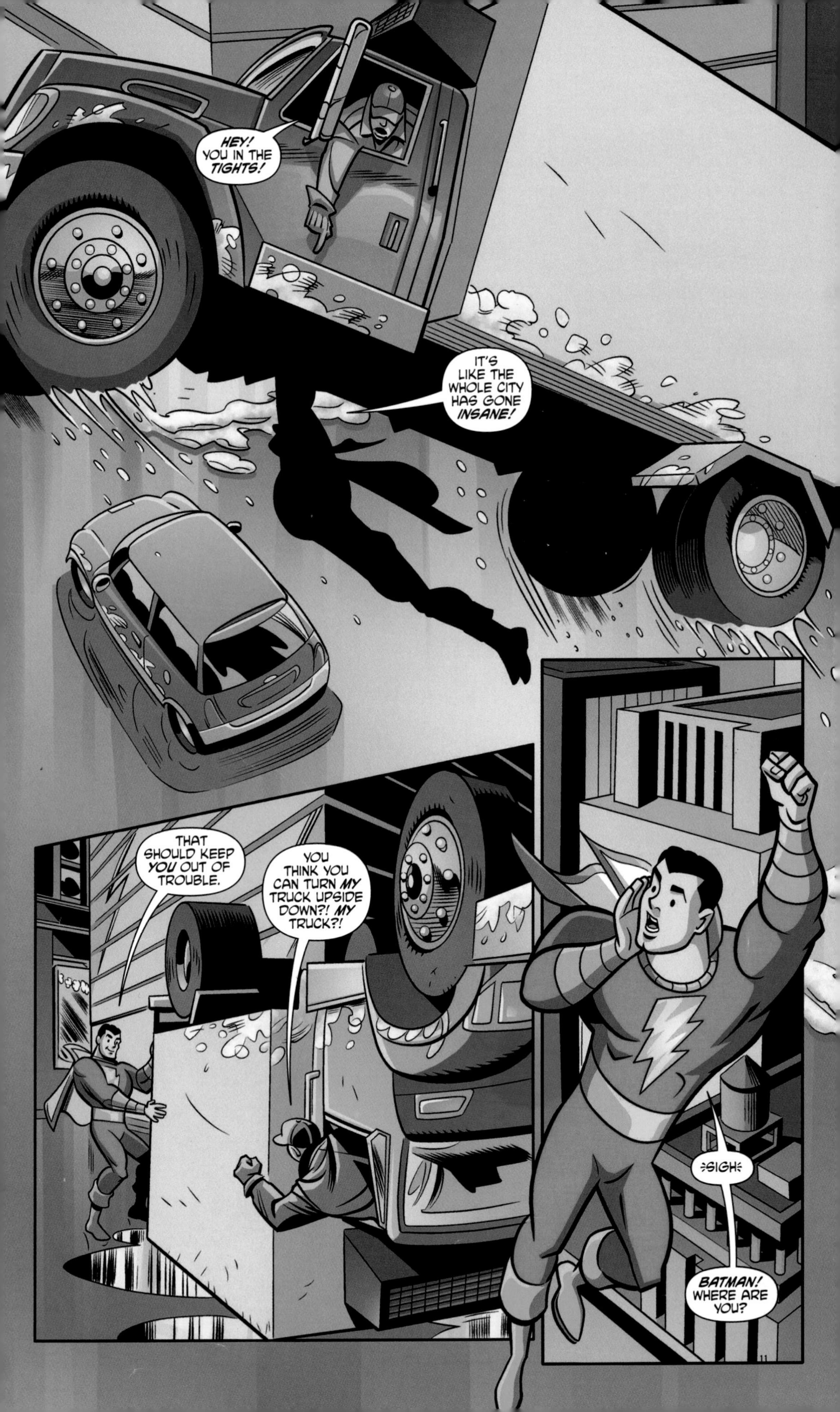
HEY! YOU IN THE TIGHTS!
IT'S LIKE THE WHOLE CITY HAS GONE INSANE!
THAT SHOULD KEEP YOU OUT OF TROUBLE.
YOU THINK YOU CAN TURN MY TRUCK UPSIDE DOWN?! MY TRUCK?!
SIGH
BATMAN! WHERE ARE YOU?

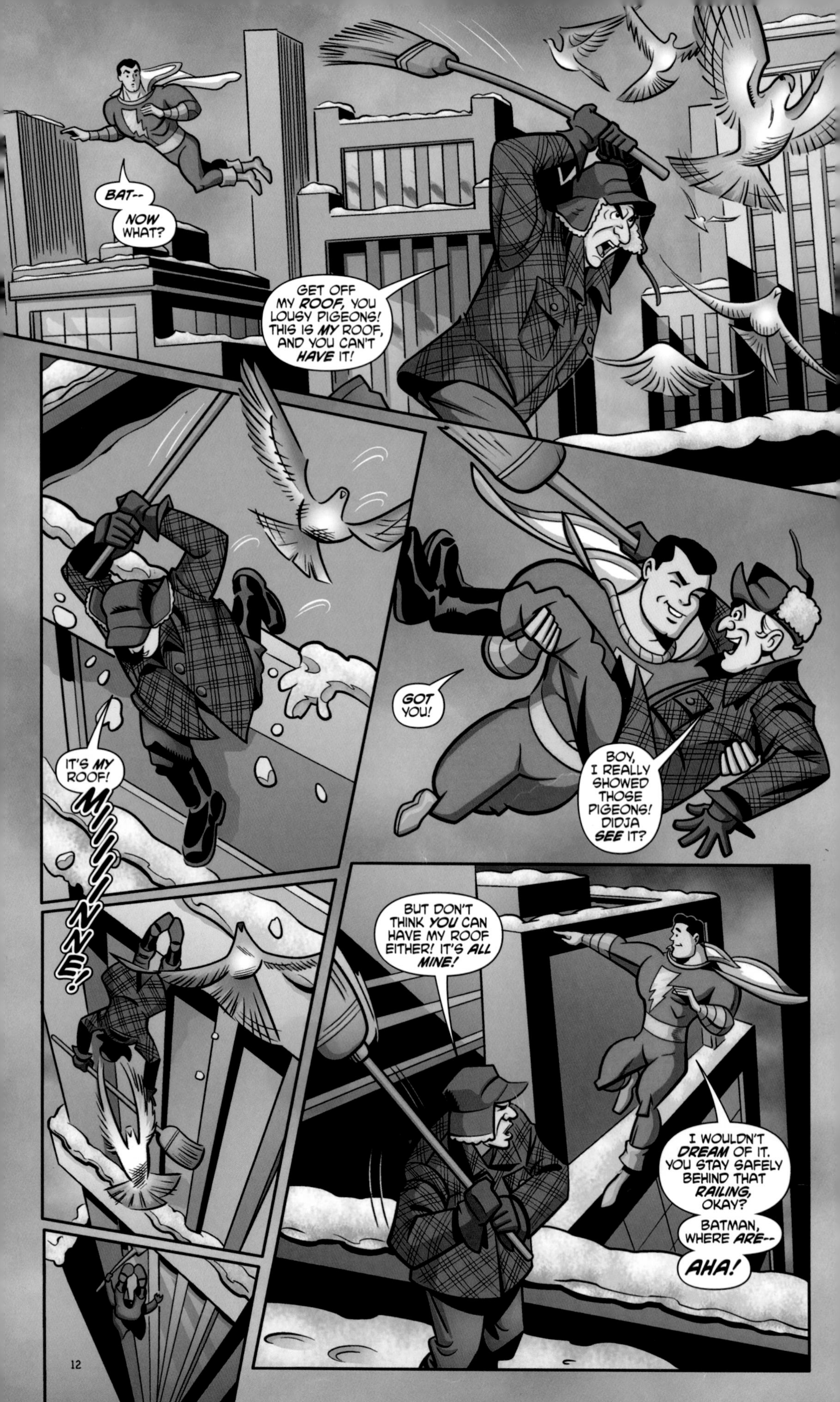

BAT-- NOW WHAT?
GET OFF MY ROOF, YOU LOUSY PIGEONS! THIS IS MY ROOF, AND YOU CAN'T HAVE IT!
IT'S MY ROOF!
MIIIIINNNE!
GOT YOU!
BOY, I REALLY SHOWED THOSE PIGEONS! DIDJA SEE IT?
BUT DON'T THINK YOU CAN HAVE MY ROOF EITHER! IT'S ALL MINE!
I WOULDN'T DREAM OF IT. YOU STAY SAFELY BEHIND THAT RAILING, OKAY?
BATMAN, WHERE ARE--
AHA!

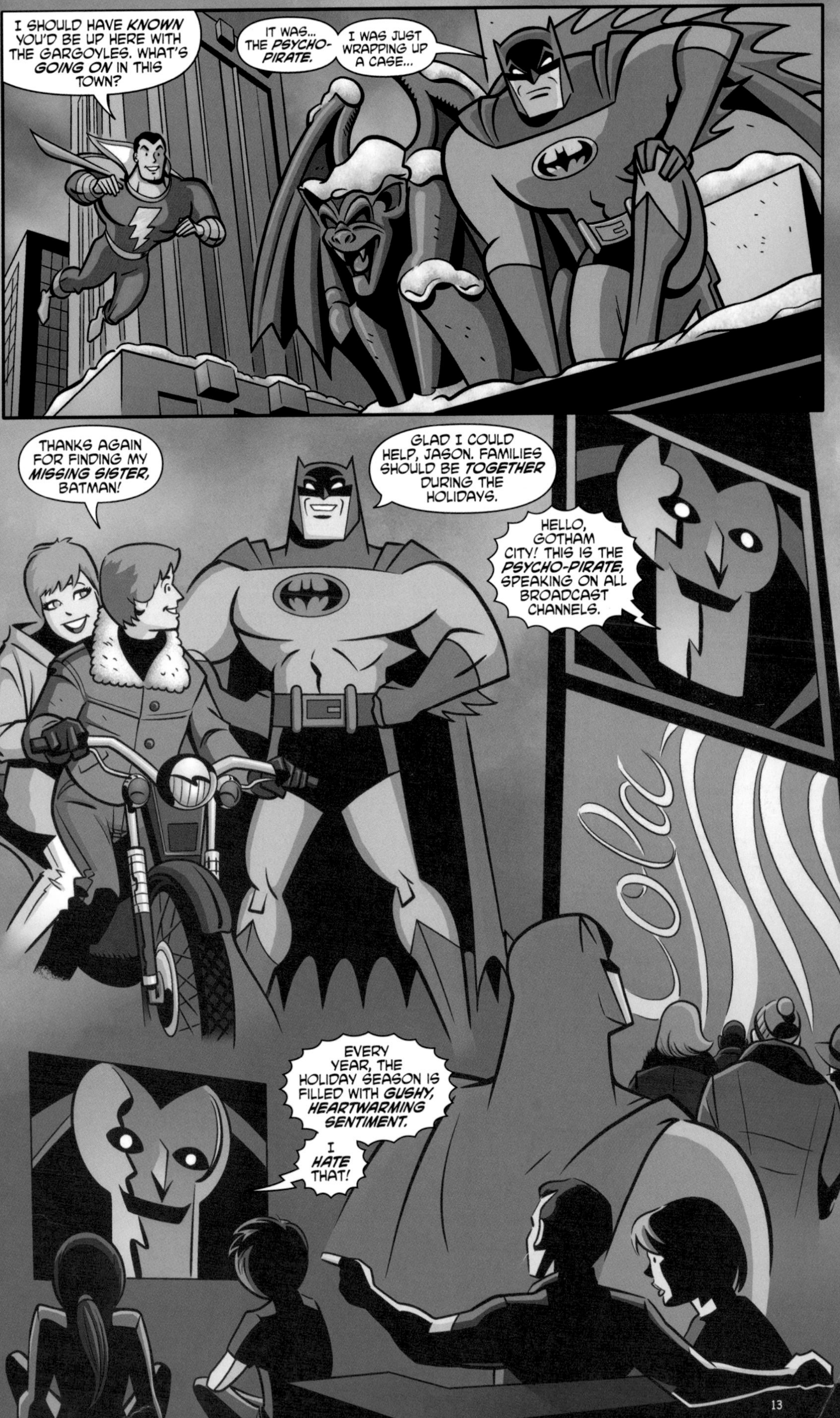

I SHOULD HAVE KNOWN YOU'D BE UP HERE WITH THE GARGOYLES. WHAT'S GOING ON IN THIS TOWN?
I WAS JUST WRAPPING UP A CASE...
IT WAS... THE PSYCHO-PIRATE.
THANKS AGAIN FOR FINDING MY MISSING SISTER, BATMAN!
GLAD I COULD HELP, JASON. FAMILIES SHOULD BE TOGETHER DURING THE HOLIDAYS.
HELLO, GOTHAM CITY! THIS IS THE PSYCHO-PIRATE, SPEAKING ON ALL BROADCAST CHANNELS.
Cola
EVERY YEAR, THE HOLIDAY SEASON IS FILLED WITH GUSHY, HEARTWARMING SENTIMENT.
I HATE THAT!

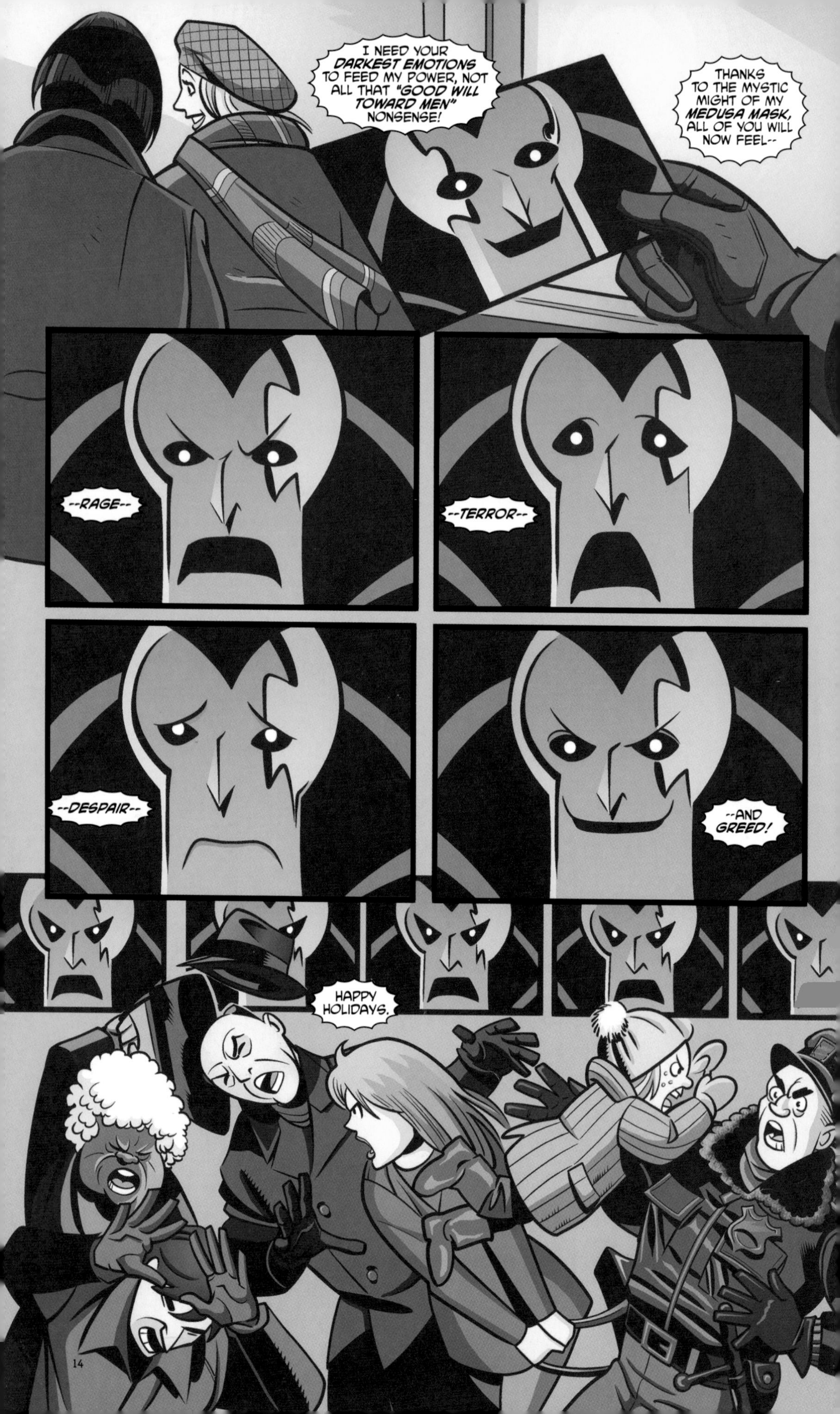
I NEED YOUR DARKEST EMOTIONS TO FEED MY POWER, NOT ALL THAT "GOOD WILL TOWARD MEN" NONSENSE!
THANKS TO THE MYSTIC MIGHT OF MY MEDUSA MASK, ALL OF YOU WILL NOW FEEL--
--RAGE--
--TERROR--
--DESPAIR--
--AND GREED!
HAPPY HOLIDAYS.

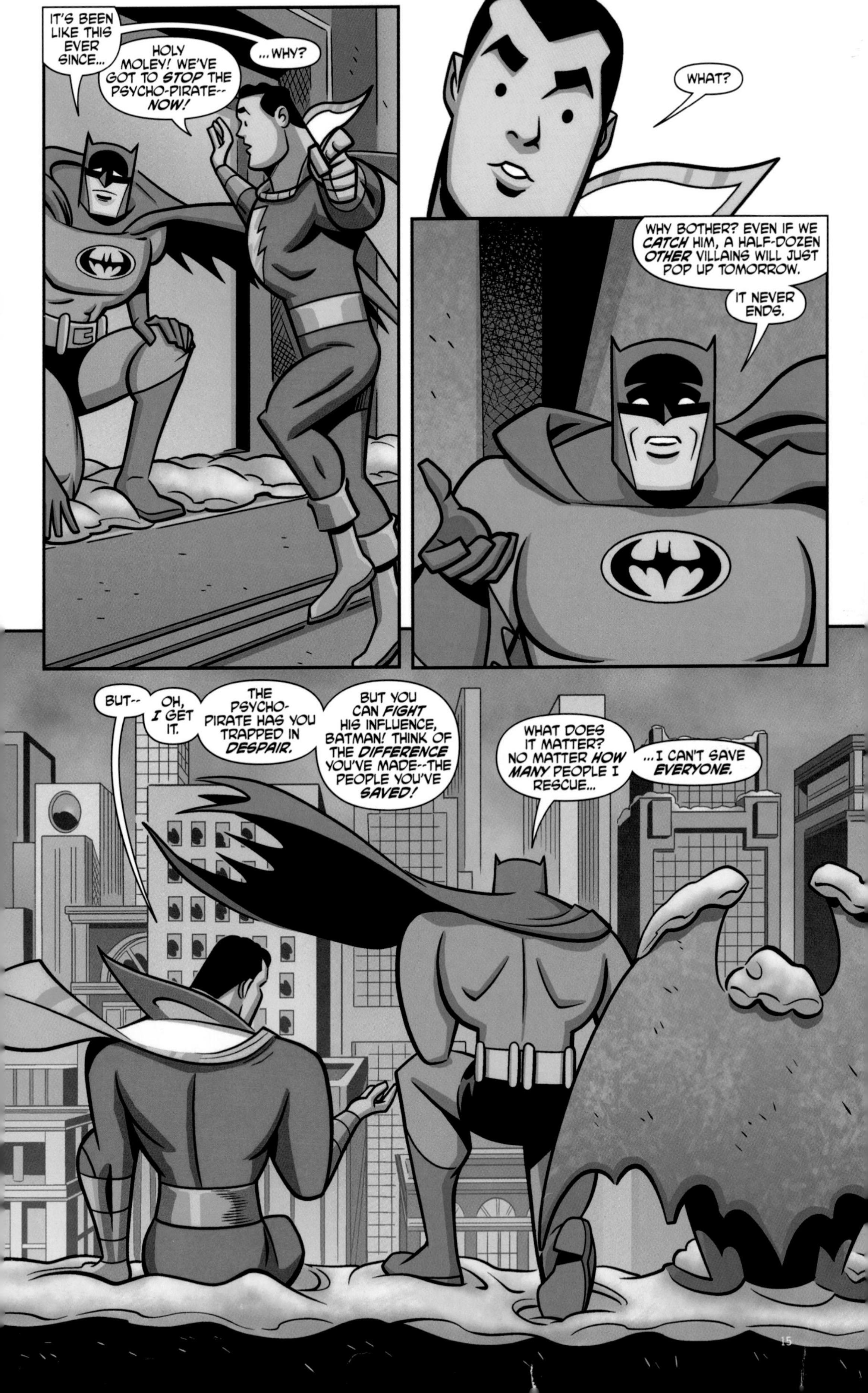
IT'S BEEN LIKE THIS EVER SINCE...
HOLY MOLEY! WE'VE GOT TO STOP THE PSYCHO-PIRATE-- NOW!
...WHY?
WHAT?
WHY BOTHER? EVEN IF WE CATCH HIM, A HALF-DOZEN OTHER VILLAINS WILL JUST POP UP TOMORROW.
IT NEVER ENDS.
BUT--
OH, I GET IT.
THE PSYCHO-PIRATE HAS YOU TRAPPED IN DESPAIR.
BUT YOU CAN FIGHT HIS INFLUENCE, BATMAN! THINK OF THE DIFFERENCE YOU'VE MADE--THE PEOPLE YOU'VE SAVED!
WHAT DOES IT MATTER? NO MATTER HOW MANY PEOPLE I RESCUE...
...I CAN'T SAVE EVERYONE.

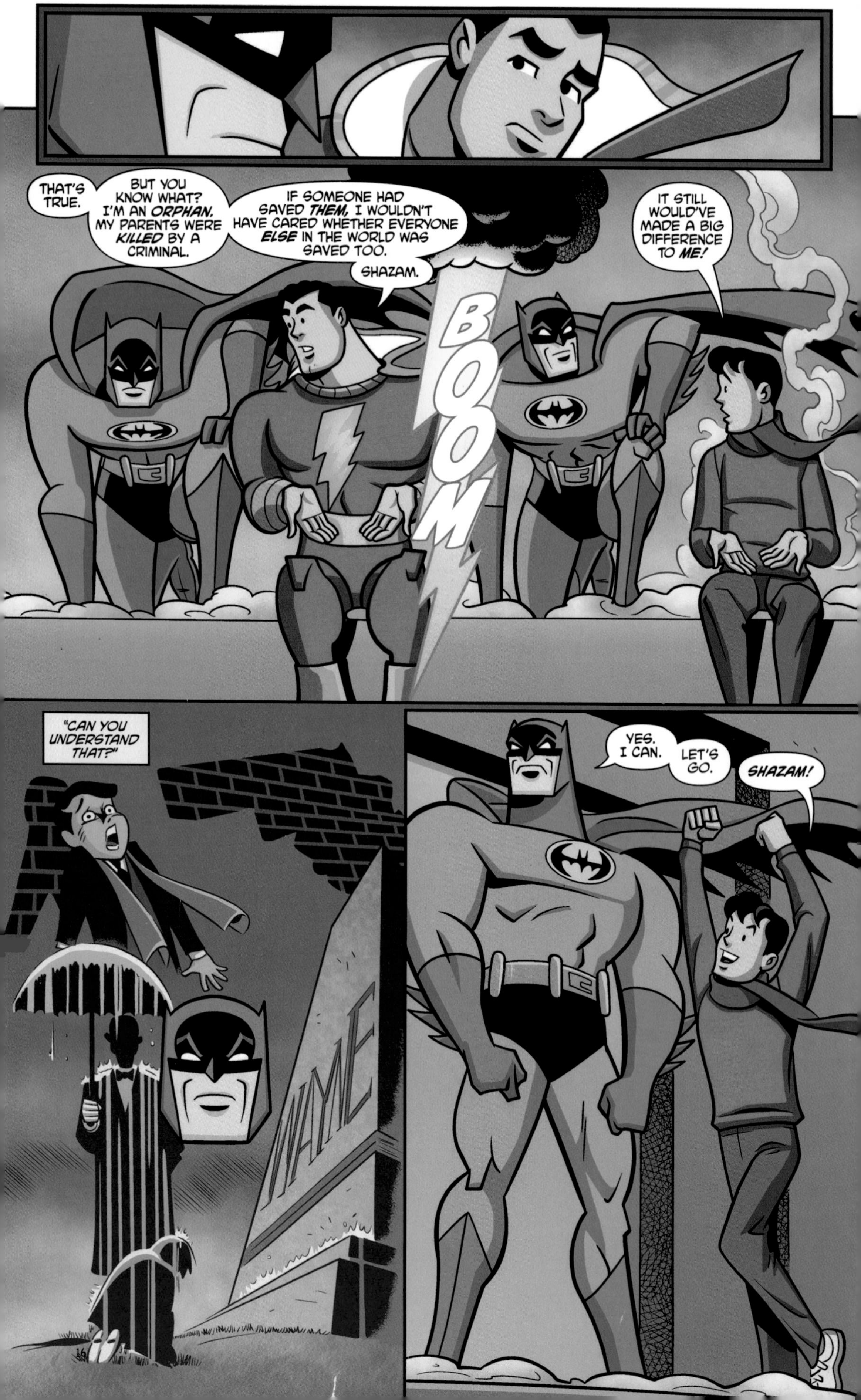
THAT'S TRUE.
BUT YOU KNOW WHAT? I'M AN ORPHAN. MY PARENTS WERE KILLED BY A CRIMINAL.
IF SOMEONE HAD SAVED THEM, I WOULDN'T HAVE CARED WHETHER EVERYONE ELSE IN THE WORLD WAS SAVED TOO.
IT STILL WOULD'VE MADE A BIG DIFFERENCE TO ME!
SHAZAM.
BOOOM
"CAN YOU UNDERSTAND THAT?"
WAYNE
YES. I CAN.
LET'S GO.
SHAZAM!

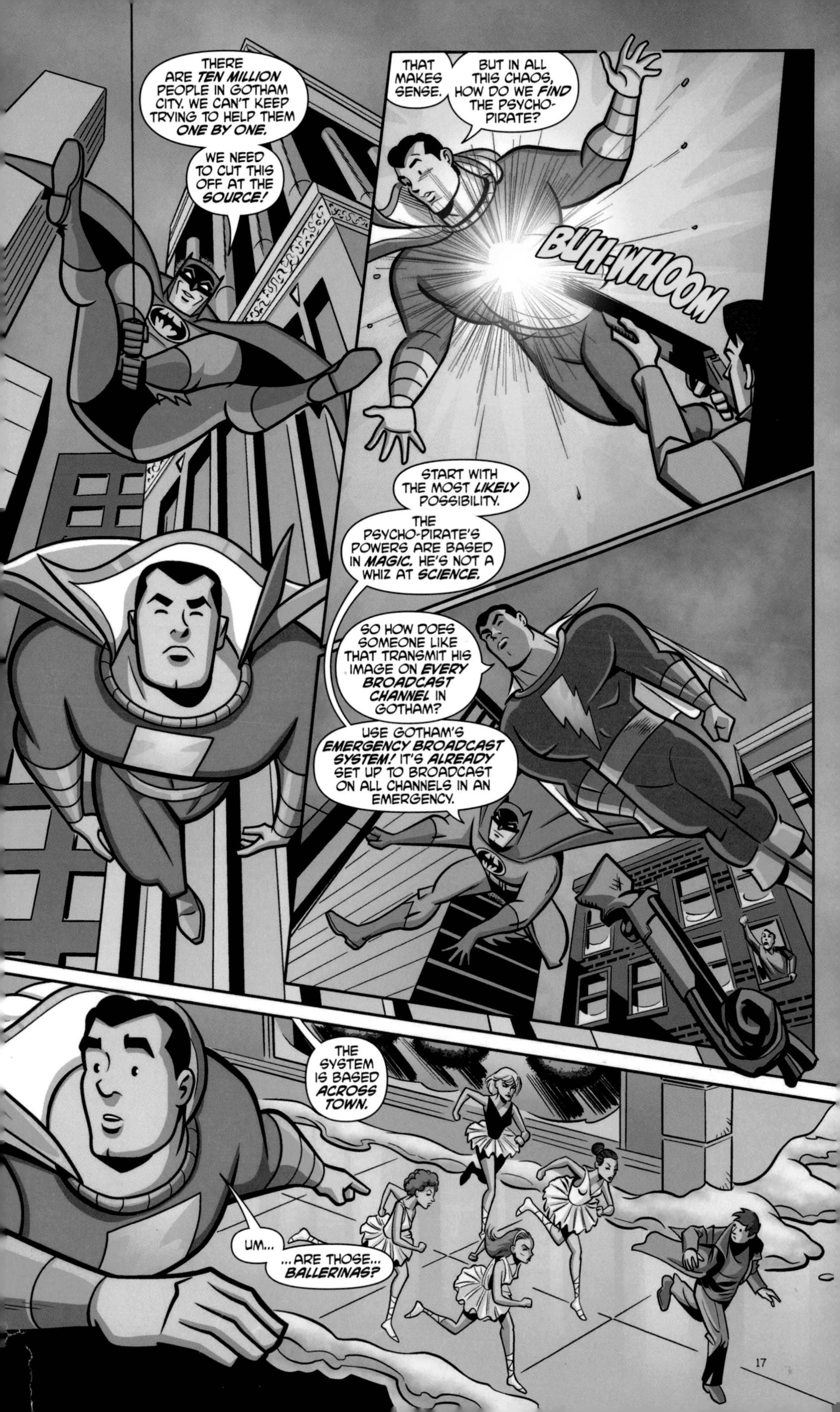

THERE ARE TEN MILLION PEOPLE IN GOTHAM CITY. WE CAN'T KEEP TRYING TO HELP THEM ONE BY ONE.
WE NEED TO CUT THIS OFF AT THE SOURCE!
THAT MAKES SENSE.
BUT IN ALL THIS CHAOS, HOW DO WE FIND THE PSYCHO-PIRATE?
BUH-WHOOM
START WITH THE MOST LIKELY POSSIBILITY.
THE PSYCHO-PIRATE'S POWERS ARE BASED IN MAGIC. HE'S NOT A WHIZ AT SCIENCE.
SO HOW DOES SOMEONE LIKE THAT TRANSMIT HIS IMAGE ON EVERY BROADCAST CHANNEL IN GOTHAM?
USE GOTHAM'S EMERGENCY BROADCAST SYSTEM! IT'S ALREADY SET UP TO BROADCAST ON ALL CHANNELS IN AN EMERGENCY.
THE SYSTEM IS BASED ACROSS TOWN.
UM...
...ARE THOSE... BALLERINAS?

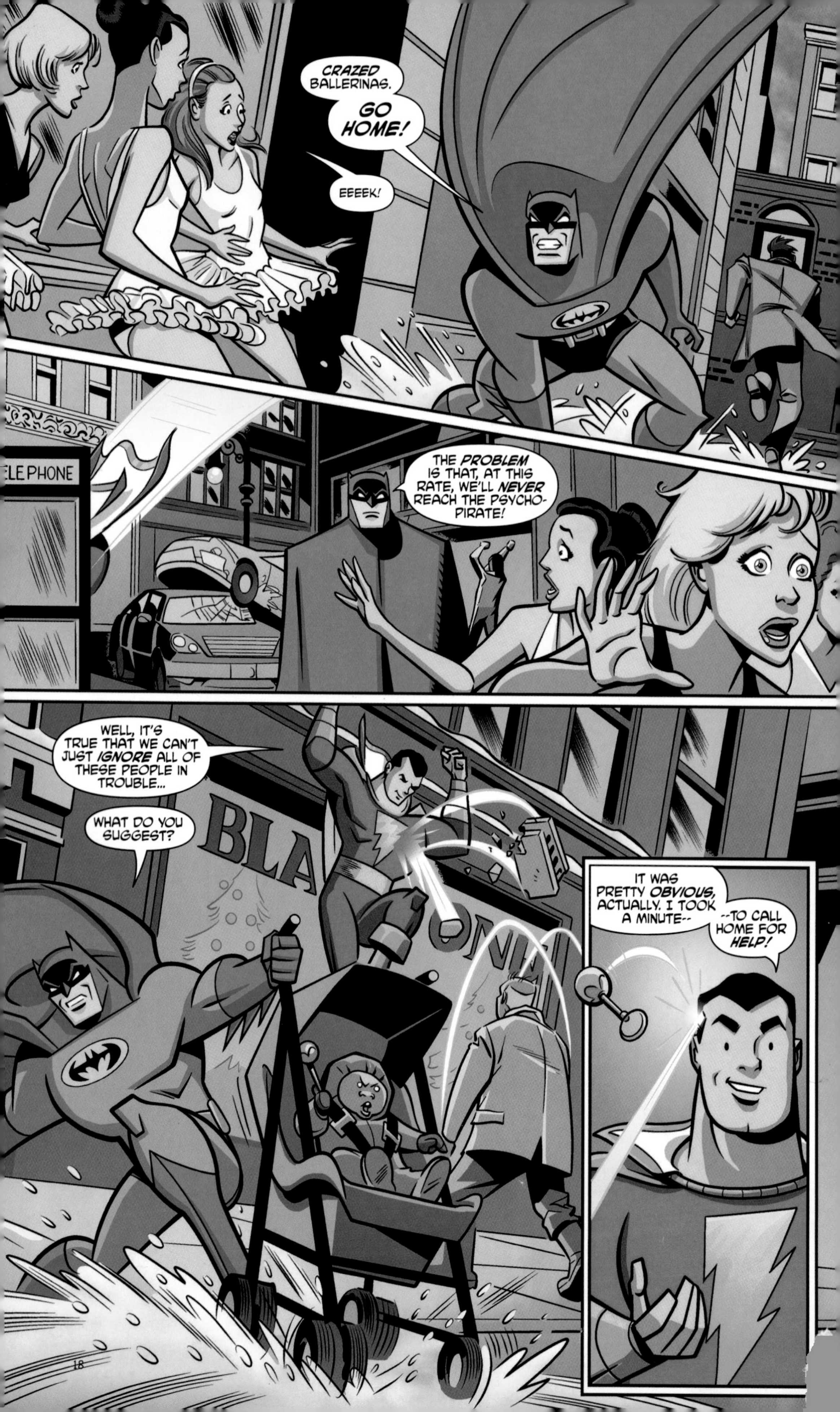
CRAZED BALLERINAS.
GO HOME!
EEEEK!
ELEPHONE
THE PROBLEM IS THAT, AT THIS RATE, WE'LL NEVER REACH THE PSYCHO-PIRATE!
WELL, IT'S TRUE THAT WE CAN'T JUST IGNORE ALL OF THESE PEOPLE IN TROUBLE...
WHAT DO YOU SUGGEST?
BLA
IT WAS PRETTY OBVIOUS, ACTUALLY. I TOOK A MINUTE--
--TO CALL HOME FOR HELP!

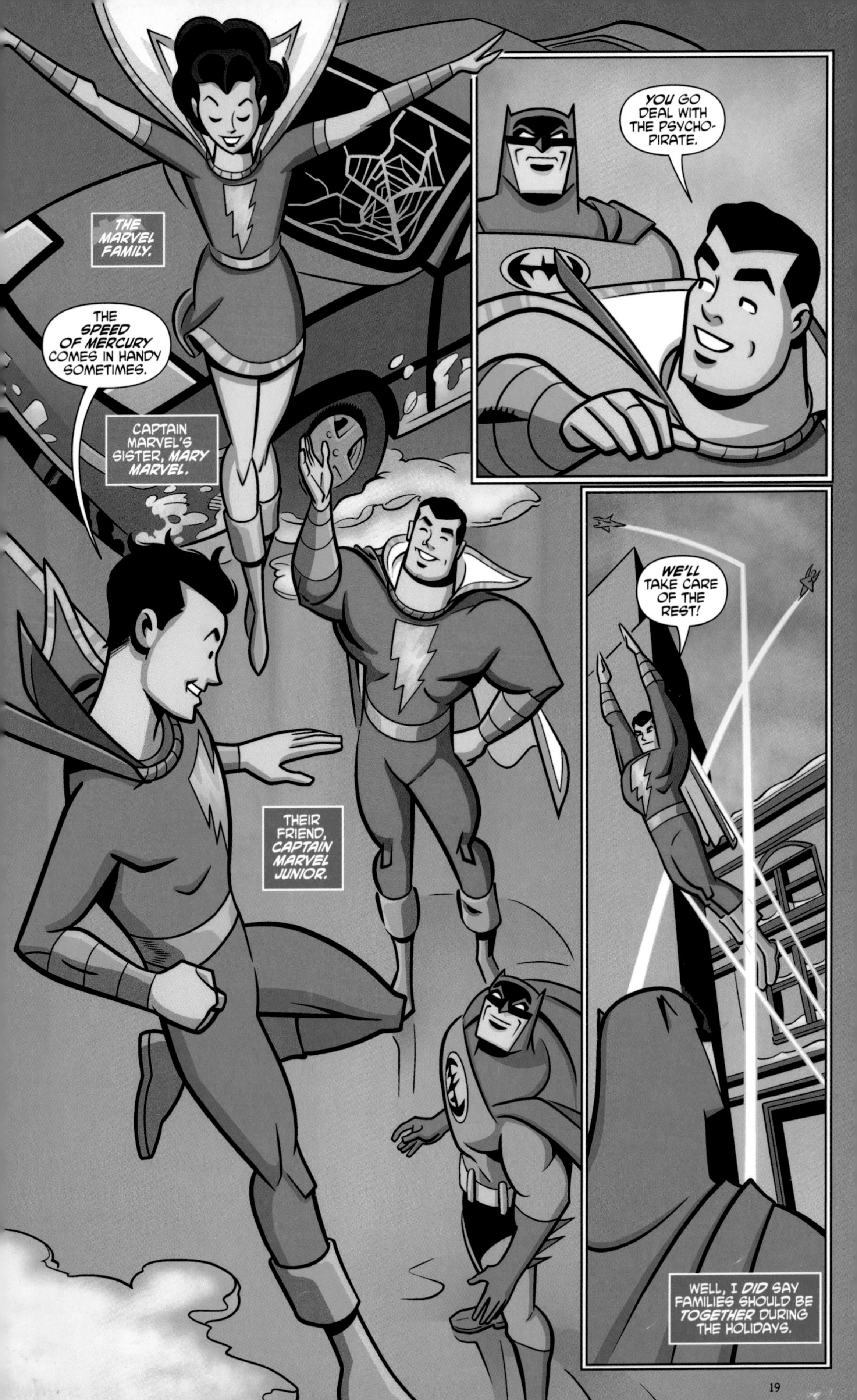

THE MARVEL FAMILY.
THE SPEED OF MERCURY COMES IN HANDY SOMETIMES.
CAPTAIN MARVEL'S SISTER, MARY MARVEL.
THEIR FRIEND, CAPTAIN MARVEL JUNIOR.
YOU GO DEAL WITH THE PSYCHO-PIRATE.
WE'LL TAKE CARE OF THE REST!
WELL, I DID SAY FAMILIES SHOULD BE TOGETHER DURING THE HOLIDAYS.

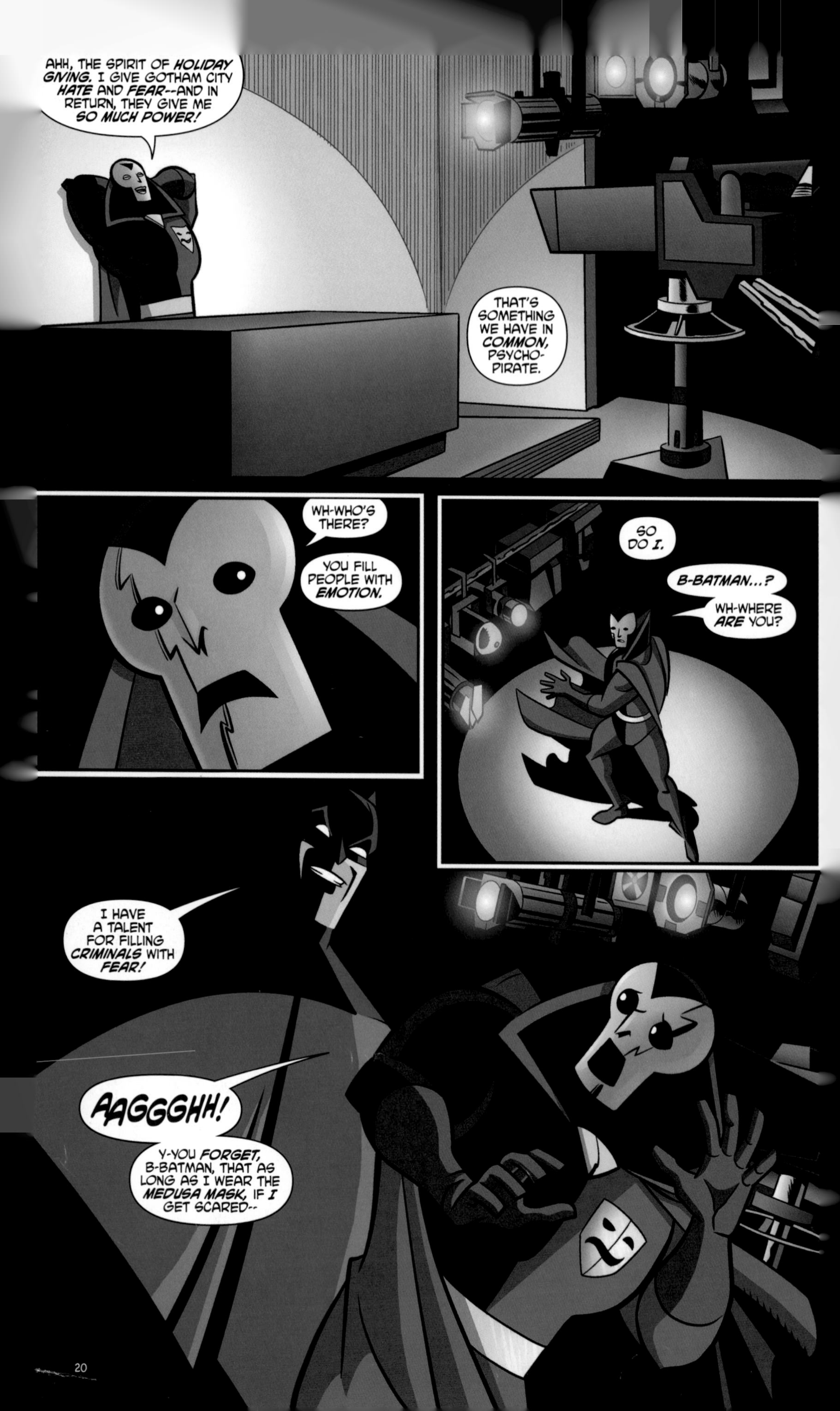
AHH, THE SPIRIT OF HOLIDAY GIVING. I GIVE GOTHAM CITY HATE AND FEAR--AND IN RETURN, THEY GIVE ME SO MUCH POWER!
THAT'S SOMETHING WE HAVE IN COMMON, PSYCHO-PIRATE.
WH-WHO'S THERE?
YOU FILL PEOPLE WITH EMOTION.
SO DO I.
B-BATMAN...?
WH-WHERE ARE YOU?
I HAVE A TALENT FOR FILLING CRIMINALS WITH FEAR!
AAGGGHH!
Y-YOU FORGET, B-BATMAN, THAT AS LONG AS I WEAR THE MEDUSA MASK, IF I GET SCARED--

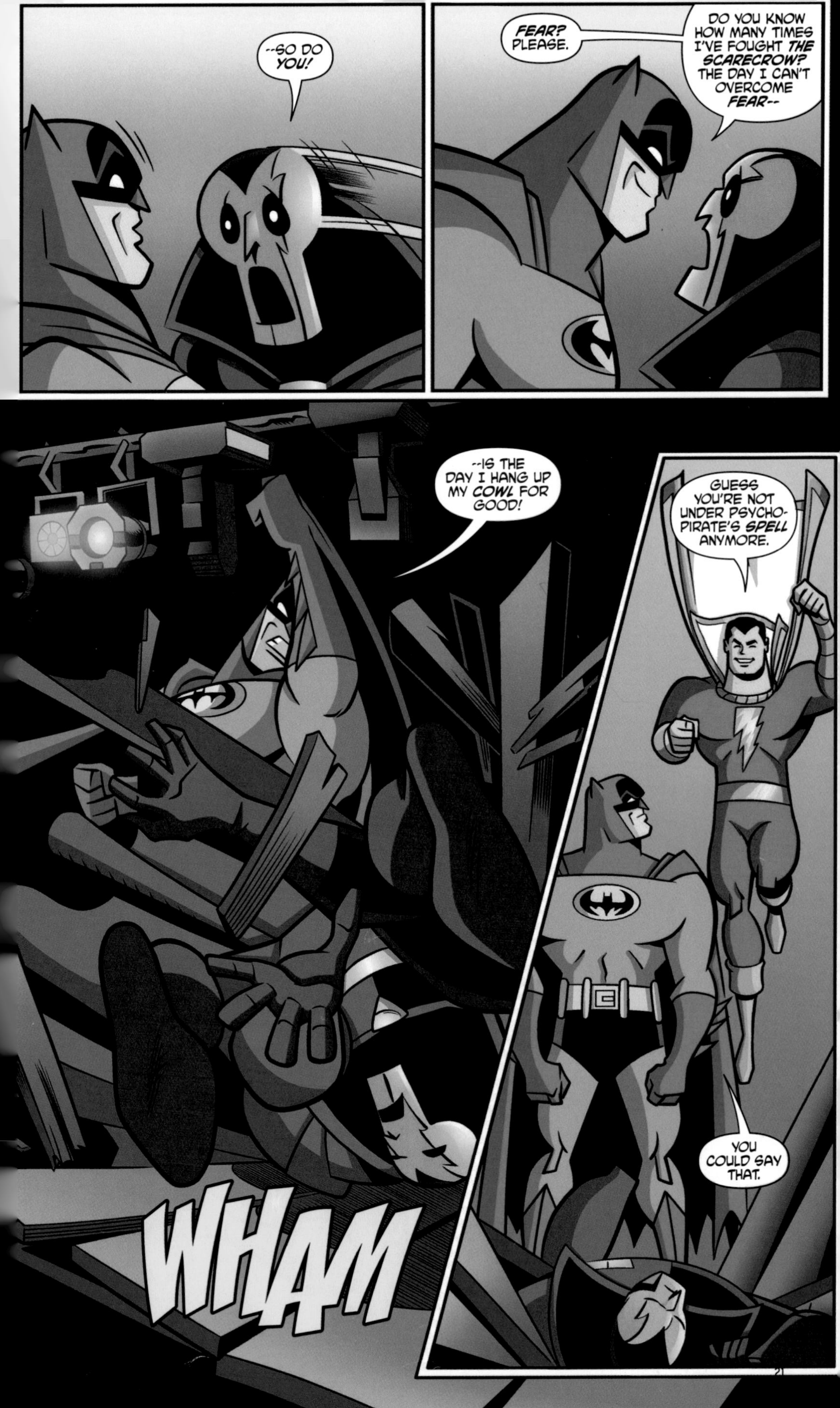
--SO DO YOU!
FEAR? PLEASE.
DO YOU KNOW HOW MANY TIMES I'VE FOUGHT THE SCARECROW? THE DAY I CAN'T OVERCOME FEAR--
--IS THE DAY I HANG UP MY COWL FOR GOOD!
WHAM
GUESS YOU'RE NOT UNDER PSYCHO-PIRATE'S SPELL ANYMORE.
YOU COULD SAY THAT.

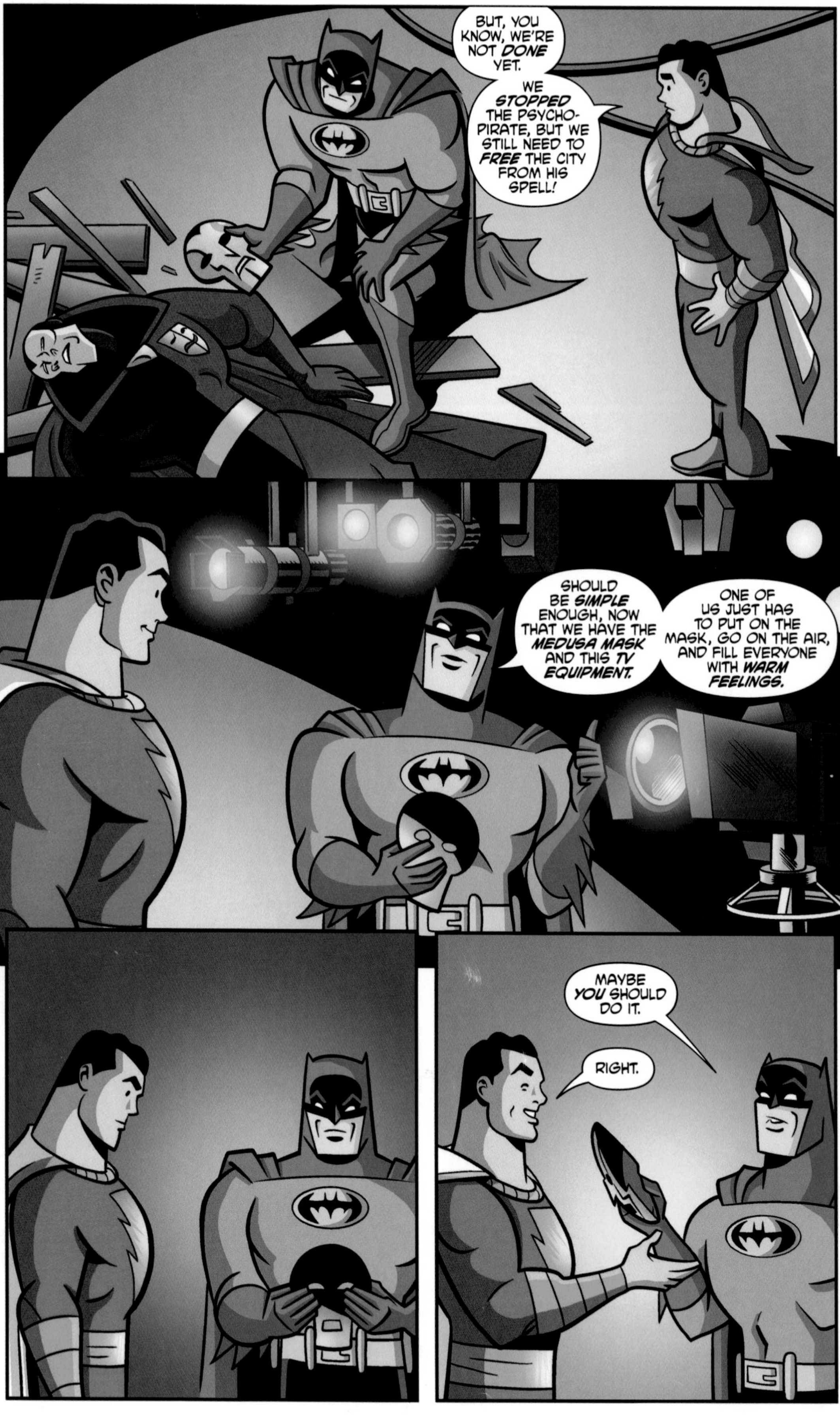

BUT, YOU KNOW, WE'RE NOT DONE YET.
WE STOPPED THE PSYCHO-PIRATE, BUT WE STILL NEED TO FREE THE CITY FROM HIS SPELL!
SHOULD BE SIMPLE ENOUGH, NOW THAT WE HAVE THE MEDUSA MASK AND THIS TV EQUIPMENT.
ONE OF US JUST HAS TO PUT ON THE MASK, GO ON THE AIR, AND FILL EVERYONE WITH WARM FEELINGS.
MAYBE YOU SHOULD DO IT.
RIGHT.

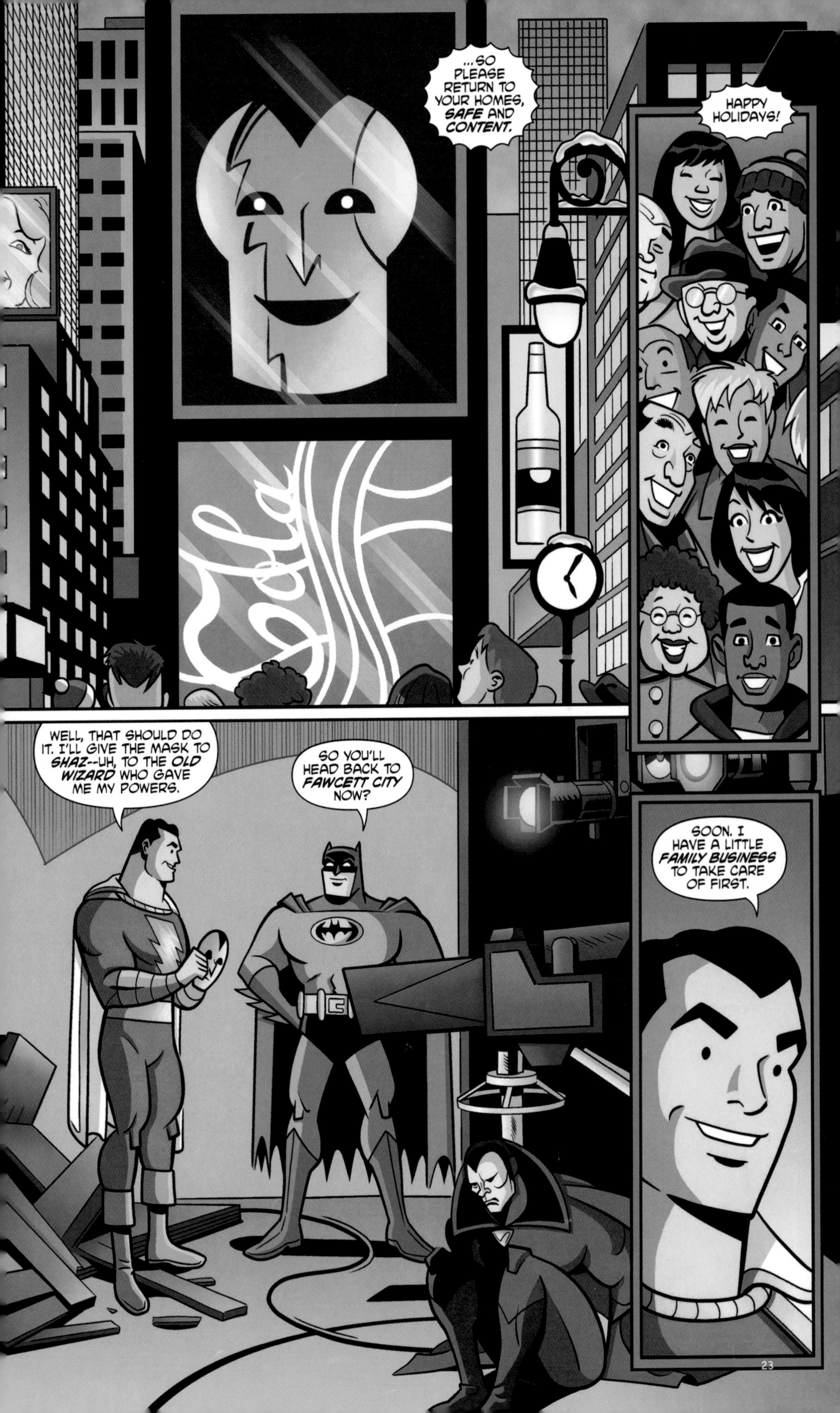

...SO PLEASE RETURN TO YOUR HOMES, SAFE AND CONTENT.
HAPPY HOLIDAYS!
WELL, THAT SHOULD DO IT. I'LL GIVE THE MASK TO SHAZ--UH, TO THE OLD WIZARD WHO GAVE ME MY POWERS.
SO YOU'LL HEAD BACK TO FAWCETT CITY NOW?
SOON. I HAVE A LITTLE FAMILY BUSINESS TO TAKE CARE OF FIRST.

CAPTAIN MARVEL HAS MANY *SUPER POWERS.*

THE *WISDOM* OF SOLOMON. THE *STRENGTH* OF HERCULES.

THE *STAMINA* OF ATLAS. THE *POWER* OF ZEUS.

THE *COURAGE* OF ACHILLES. THE *SPEED* OF MERCURY.

OH, *THERE* YOU ARE.

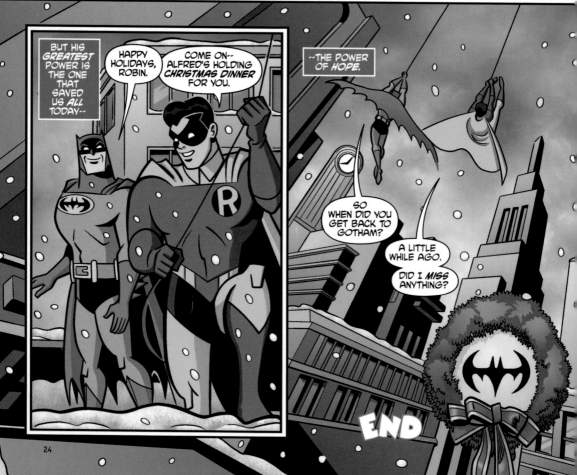

BUT HIS *GREATEST* POWER IS THE ONE THAT SAVED US *ALL* TODAY--

HAPPY HOLIDAYS, ROBIN.

COME ON-- ALFRED'S HOLDING *CHRISTMAS DINNER* FOR YOU.

--THE POWER OF *HOPE.*

SO WHEN DID YOU GET BACK TO *GOTHAM?*

A LITTLE WHILE AGO.

DID I *MISS* ANYTHING?

END

CREATORS

SHOLLY FISCH
WRITER

Bitten by a radioactive typewriter, Sholly Fisch has spent the wee hours writing books, comics, TV scripts, and online material for over 25 years. His comic book credits include more than 200 stories and features about characters such as Batman, Superman, Bugs Bunny, Daffy Duck, Spider-Man, and Ben 10. Currently, he writes stories for Action Comics every month, plus stories for Looney Tunes and Scooby-Doo. By day, Sholly is a mild-mannered developmental psychologist who helps to create educational TV shows, websites, and other media for kids.

RICK BURCHETT
PENCILLER

Rick Burchett has worked as a comics artist for over 25 years. He has received the comics industry's Eisner Award three times, Spain's Haxtur Award, and he has been nominated for England's Eagle Award. Rick lives with his wife and two sons near St. Louis, Missouri.

DAN DAVIS
INKER

Dan Davis has illustrated the Garfield comic series as well as books for Warner Bros. and DC Comics. He has brought a variety of comic book characters to life, including Batman and the rest of the Super Friends! In 2012, Dan was nominated for an Eisner Award for the Batman: The Brave and the Bold series. He currently resides in Gotham City.

GLOSSARY

broadcast [BRAWD·kast]--to send out a radio or television program to an audience

chaos [KAY·oss]--complete confusion

cowl [COW·uhl]--a long, hooded cloak

despair [di·SPAIR]--extreme sadness

gargoyle [GHAR·goil]--an animal figure carved out of stone and used to carry rainwater away from a building

heartwarming [HAHRT·warm·ing]--making someone feel good

influence [IN·floo·uhnss]--an effect on someone or something

insane [in·SANE]--mentally ill or very foolish

overcome [oh·vur·KUHM]--to conquer or defeat

restrain [ri·STRAYN]--to hold back or keep under control

sentiment [SEN·tuh·muhnt]--an opinion or a sensitive feeling

stamina [STAM·uh·nuh]--the energy or strength to keep doing something

VISUAL QUESTIONS & PROMPTS

1. Why do you think the artist drew two different expressions for Billy and Mr. Tawny side by side? What's happening to Billy? What's happening to Mr. Tawny?

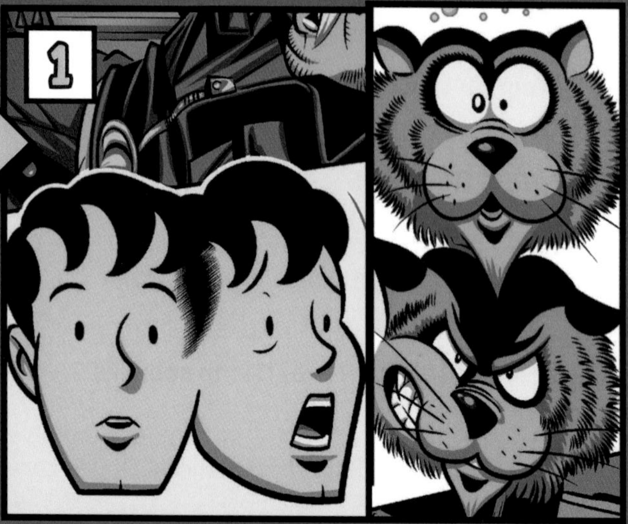
1

2. Psycho-Pirate makes everyone feel negative emotions in order to strengthen his power. What kind of emotions might make him weaker?

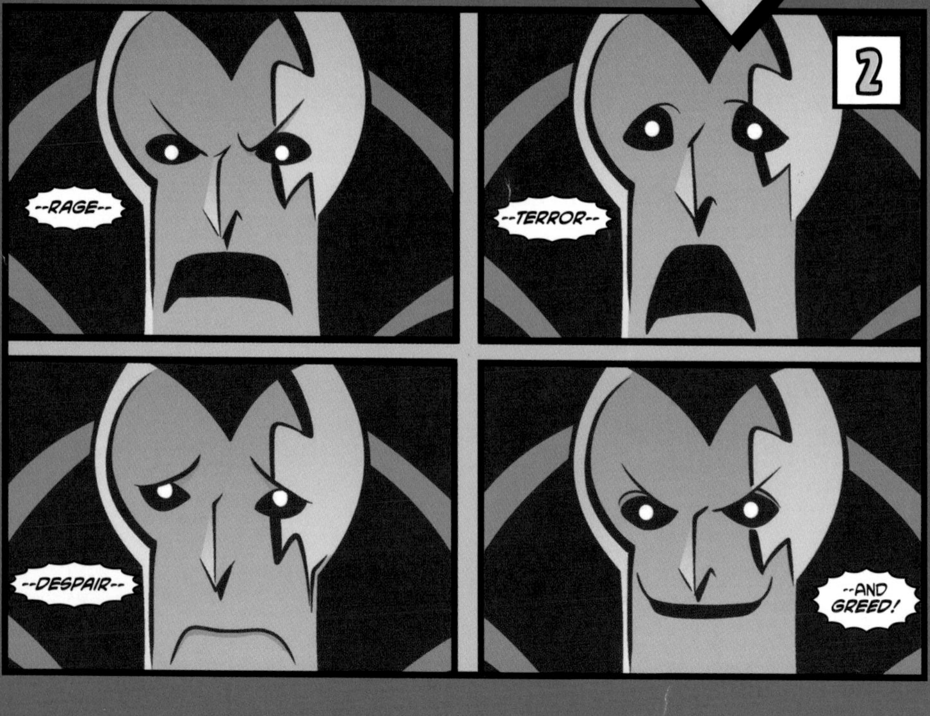
2
--RAGE--
--TERROR--
--DESPAIR--
--AND GREED!

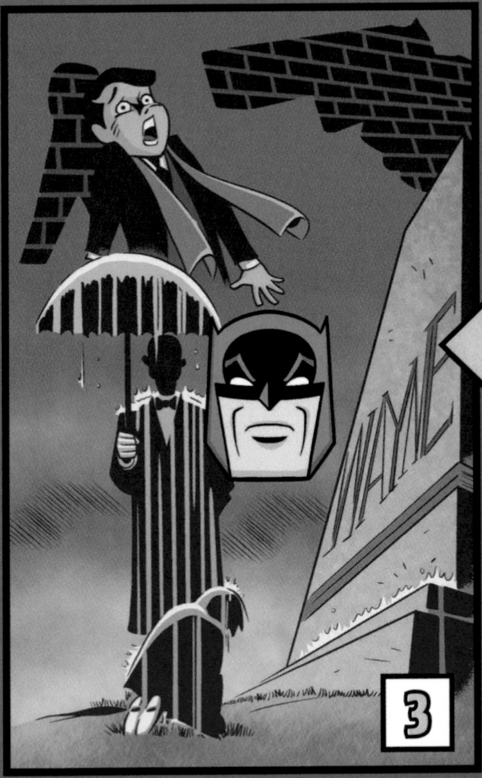
WAYNE
3

3. Artists use different techniques to let us know that something is occurring in the past. What clues does the artist give us in this panel to let us know that the scene is not occurring in the present?

4. When the story begins, everyone in Gotham is already unhappy. Captain Marvel and Batman are able to cure everyone's unhappiness by defeating Psycho-Pirate. How would the story be different if it began with everyone being happy and ended with everyone in despair?

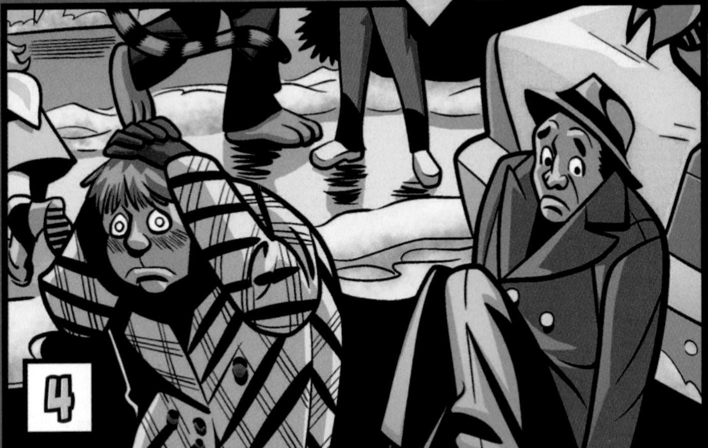
4

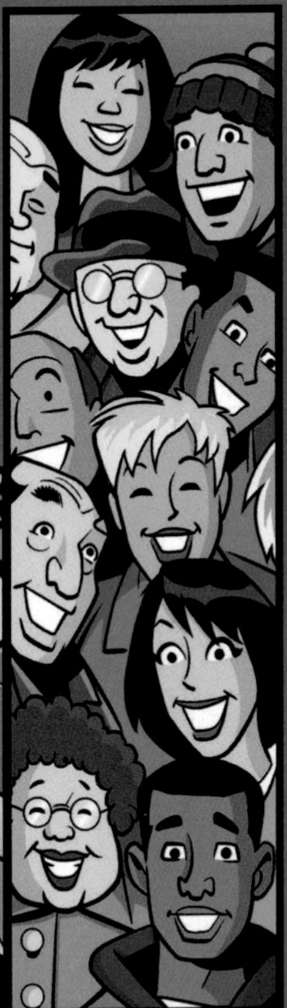

READ THEM ALL!

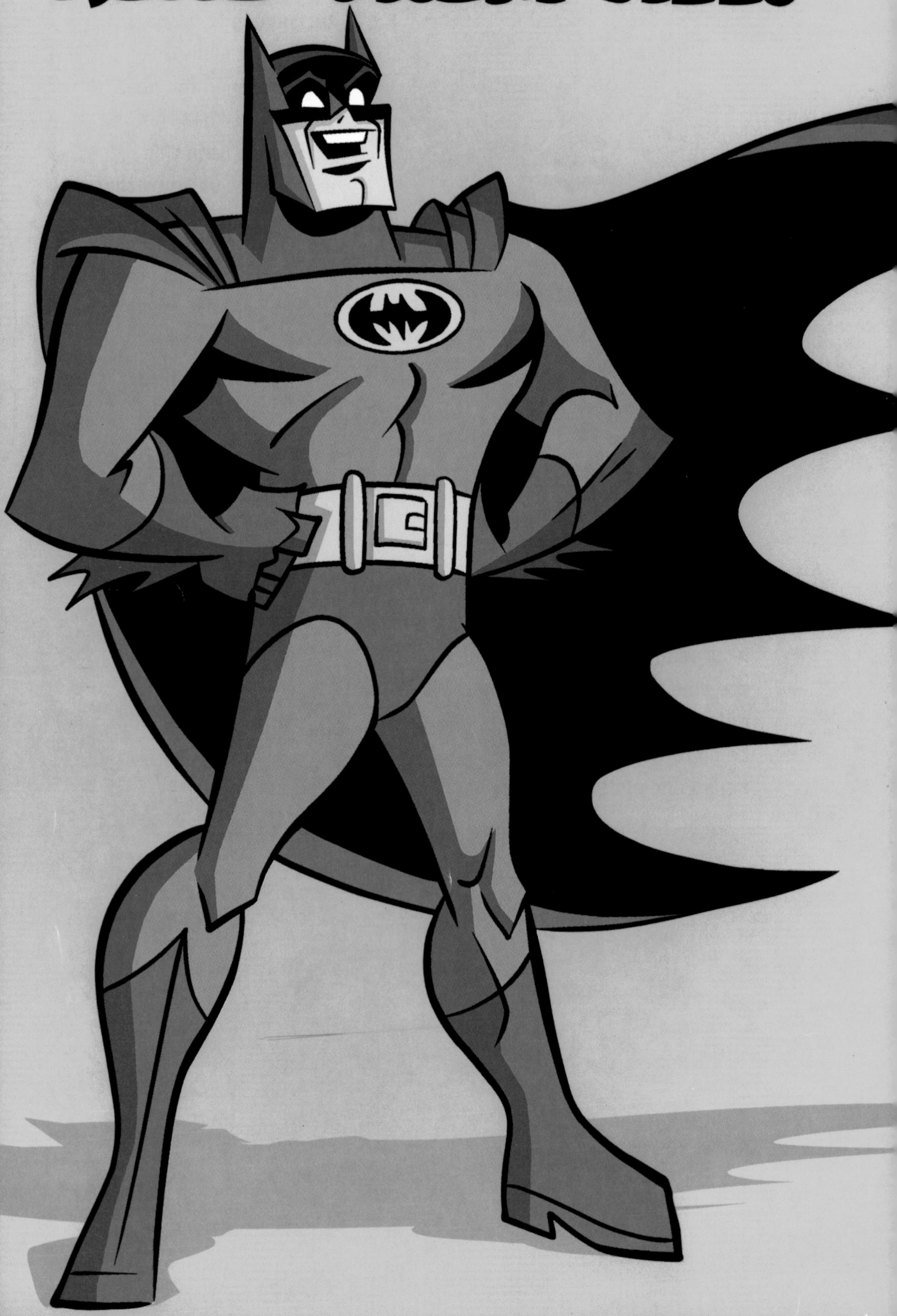

THE ALL NEW! BATMAN

THE BRAVE AND THE BOLD

THE ALL NEW!
BATMAN
THE BRAVE AND THE BOLD
DC COMICS
BATTLE OF THE PLANETS
FISCH
BURCHETT
DAVIS

THE ALL NEW!
BATMAN
THE BRAVE AND THE BOLD
DC COMICS
THAT HOLIDAY FEELING
FISCH
BURCHETT
DAVIS

THE ALL NEW!
BATMAN
THE BRAVE AND THE BOLD
DC COMICS
THROUGH THE LOOKING GLASS
FISCH
BURCHETT
DAVIS

THE ALL NEW!
BATMAN
THE BRAVE AND THE BOLD
DC COMICS
FISCH
BURCHETT
DAVIS
THE BRIDE AND THE BOLD

THE ALL NEW!
BATMAN
THE BRAVE AND THE BOLD
DC COMICS
FISCH
BURCHETT
DAVIS
MANHANDLED BY MANHUNTERS!

THE ALL NEW!
BATMAN
THE BRAVE AND THE BOLD
DC COMICS
FISCH
BURCHETT
DAVIS
CLOBBERED BY CLAYFACE!

THE ALL NEW!

BATMAN

THE BRAVE AND THE BOLD

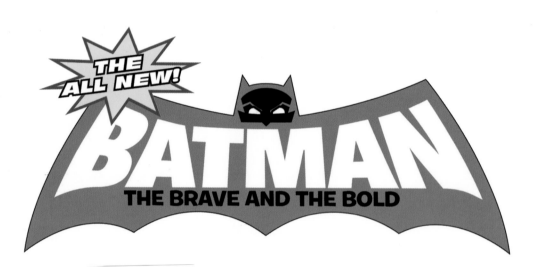